THE BREAST

THE BREAST

PHILIP ROTH

JONATHAN CAPE
THIRTY BEDFORD SQUARE LONDON

FIRST PUBLISHED IN GREAT BRITAIN 1973
COPYRIGHT © 1973 BY PHILIP ROTH

JONATHAN CAPE LTD, 30 BEDFORD SQUARE, LONDON WCI

ISBN 0 224 00810 2

PRINTED IN GREAT BRITAIN BY
LOWE AND BRYDONE (PRINTERS) LTD, LONDON
ON PAPER MADE BY JOHN DICKINSON & CO. LTD
BOUND BY G AND J KITCAT LTD, LONDON

To *Elizabeth Ames,* executive director
of Yaddo from 1924 to 1970,
and to *The Corporation of Yaddo,*
Saratoga Springs, New York,
the best friends a writer could have

THE BREAST

It began oddly. But could it have begun otherwise, however it began? It has been said, of course, that everything under the sun begins "oddly" and ends "oddly" and *is* "odd": a perfect rose is "odd," so is an imperfect rose, so is the rose of ordinary rosy good looks growing in your neighbor's garden. I know about the perspective from which everything appears awesome and mysterious. Reflect upon eternity, consider, if you are up to it, oblivion, and everything that is is a wonder. Still and all I would submit to you, in all humility, that some things are more wondrous than others, and I am one such thing.

It began oddly, then, with a mild, sporadic tingling in the groin. During that first week I would retire several times a day to the men's room adjacent to my office in the humanities building to take down my trousers, but upon examining myself, saw nothing out of the ordinary, assiduous as was my search. I

3

decided reluctantly, half-heartedly (and not really) to ignore it. I had been so devout a hypochondriac all my life, so alert to every change in body temperature and systemic regularity, that it had long ago become impossible for the reasonable man that I also happened to be, to take seriously the telltale symptoms that I found on myself almost weekly, invariably signs of grave and incurable disease. Despite the grim premonitions of extinction, or paralysis, or unendurable pain that would accompany each new ache or fever, I had after all to admit that I had made it to thirty-eight without any history of major illness; I was a man of hearty bowel movements, dependable sexual potency, of stamina and appetite, a man six feet tall with good posture and a trim physique, most of his hair and all of his teeth. Consequently, though I might, in self-dramatizing hypochondriacal fashion, identify this tingling in my groin with some nervous disease on the order of shingles—only worse—I simultaneously realized that it was undoubtedly, as always, nothing.

I was wrong. It was something. Another week passed before I was able to discern a pinkening of the skin just barely perceptible beneath my corkscrewed black pubic curls; the discoloration was so faint, however, that I believed I had to be imagining things. Another week again—making, for the record, an "incubation" period of twenty-one days—before I looked down at myself one evening upon stepping into the shower and discovered that somehow through that long hectic day of teaching and conferences and commuting and dining out, the flesh at the base of my penis had turned a soft reddish shade. I looked stained, as though a small raspberry, or maybe a cherry, had been crushed against my pubes, the juices running down onto my member, coloring the root of it raggedly but unmistakably *red*. Dye, I decided in the next instant, from my undershorts (that the undershorts I had worn that day had been a pale blue and lay at my feet meant nothing in that rush of panic-stricken disbelief). In the shower I lathered and rinsed my penis and my pubic hair three times over, then coated myself from the thighs to the navel with a deep icing of soap bubbles; when I rinsed with hot water—uncomfortably hot this time—the stain was still there. Not a rash, not a scab, not a bruise or a sore, but a deep pigment change such as I associated at once with cancer.

I immediately telephoned my physician at his home. Dr. Gordon is a meticulous and conscientious man, and despite my attempt to hide my alarm he heard the fear in my voice and volunteered to dress and come across town to my apartment to examine me. It was just midnight, according to the magically minded the time at which transformations take place, and a hard hour to get a doctor out in New York City. Perhaps if Claire had been with me that night, instead of back at her own apartment preparing some sort of committee report, I would have had the courage of my fear and told the doctor to come running. Of course it is unlikely that on the basis of my symptoms at that hour, Dr. Gordon would have decided to admit me to a hospital, nor would it appear from what we now know—or continue not to know—that once I was into a hospital, anything could have been done to prevent or arrest the disaster. The pain and the terror of the next four hours could perhaps have been alleviated by morphine, but nothing indicates that the process itself could have been reversed by any medical procedure short of euthanasia.

With Claire at my side, then, I might have been able to cave in completely, but alone I suddenly felt ashamed and unmanned by the way I had lost control of myself; it was no more than three minutes since I'd spotted the stain, and there I was, wet and nude on my leather sofa, trying vainly to overcome the tremolo in my voice as I looked down at my penis and gave the doctor a description of what I saw. *Take hold,* I thought—and so I took hold, as I can when I tell myself to. I said that if it was what I feared in the first startling moment, it could wait until morning; and if it wasn't it could also wait. I would be fine. I was exhausted from a hard day, I had just been—shocked. I would see him in his office at—I thought this brave of me—about noon. Nine, he said. I agreed and said, evenly as I could, "Good night."

On the phone I had recounted to the doctor the history of the tingling sensation in the groin, and had described my discolored penis with what I hoped would sound something like "medical" objectivity. I had not mentioned a third symptom, because until I hung up I had not associated it with my "condition." That was the dramatic increase in local sensation that I had experienced while making love to Claire during the preceding three weeks. I had so far associated it with a resurgence of my desire for her. From where and why I could not say—to me she was no more nor less voluptuous and lovely a young woman than she had always been—but I was delighted to have it back again. As it was, the strong lust that her physical beauty had aroused in me during the first two years of our affair had been steadily on the wane for a year now until, lately, I had come to make love to her two, maybe three times a month, and then, as often as not, at her provocation.

My cooling down, my coldness, had been distressing to both of us, but as we have both endured considerable emotional upheaval and psychic disorientation in our lives (she as a child with bitterly antagonistic and acrimonious parents, I with an enraged wife), we were equally reluctant to take any steps towards dissolving our union because of it. Dispiriting as it surely was for a handsome young woman of twenty-five to be spurned in bed night after night, Claire displayed outwardly little of the suspiciousness or frustration or distress or anger that would have seemed, even to me who was the source of her unhappiness, justified in the circumstances. Yes, she pays a price for this "equanimity"—she is not the most expressive woman I have ever known, for all her passion in sex—but I have reached the stage in my life—that is to say, I *had*—where the calm harbor and its clear, placid waters was more to my liking than the foaming drama of the high seas. Where once I had been beguiled by spontaneity and temperament, now I found my comfort with the even-tempered and the predictable. If sometimes the unrufflable in Claire made her less responsive and various in conversation, or in company, than I would have liked her to be, I was really much too content with her dependable sobriety to be too peeved with her for lacking color. I had had enough "color," thank you: six years of it.

What so distressed *me* about my waning desire was that over the course of our three years, Claire and I had worked out a way of living together—which in part involved living separately—that provided us with the warmth and security of one another's affection and company, without the accompanying burden of dependence, or the grinding boredom, or the wild, unfocused yearning, or the round-the-clock strategies of deception, placation, and dominance that seemed to have soured all but a very few of the marriages we knew of. By virtue of her unhappy childhood Claire was as hard-headed and undeluded about marriage as I was by virtue of my own unfortunate encounter with it—singular as my experience may have been, it had nonetheless produced in me a monumental capacity for abstinence, and I swore that I would never touch the stuff again. Besides, nobody really seemed to have an arrangement as commonsensical and as gratifying as ours; we really did get on so easily and with so little strain, we liked each other so much, that it seemed to me something very like a disaster (little I knew about disaster) when, out of the blue, I began to find our love-making boring and pleasureless. A year earlier I had terminated five years of psychoanalysis with the conviction that the wounds sustained in that Grand Guignol marriage (and in the lacerating divorce) had healed over as well as they ever would; I wasn't the man I once had been, but I wasn't a bleeding buck private any longer either, my skull wrapped in bandages and beating the drum of self-pity as I limped tearfully into the analyst's office from that battlefield known as Hearth and Home. With Claire life had become orderly and stable—the first time I could say that about my life in more than a decade; I felt grounded, dug in, and permanent about myself as I hadn't since I'd been a senior in college and knew for a fact that I was a serious and intelligent person. Only now, in the midst of my plenty, there was this diminishing of desire for the very woman who had helped so to fashion my new life of contentment. It was a depressing, bewildering development, and try as I might, I seemed unable to alter it. Finally I just did not care at all about touching her or being touched. I was, in fact, scheduled to pay a visit to my former analyst to discuss with him this loss of sexual appetite for Claire when, *out of the blue again,* I was suddenly more passionate than I had ever been before with her or with anyone.

Perhaps passion isn't the right word: say, more susceptible to immediate sensual delight, purely tactile pleasure. Sex, not in the head, not in the heart, but excruciatingly in the epidermis of the penis, sex skin deep and ecstatic. In bed I found myself writhing with pleasure, clawing at the sheets and twisting my head and shoulders in a way I had previously associated more with women than with men, and women more imaginary than real. Those times I felt I simply could not endure these sensations any longer, I nearly *cried* from the pleasure, and when I came I took Claire's ear in my mouth and licked it like a dog. I licked her hair. I found myself, panting, licking my own shoulder. During the final week of my incubation period, I was on her like an animal in perpetual heat. Having lain indifferently beside her for nearly a year, I was entering now upon some new compensatory phase of erotic susceptibility and fleshly release akin to nothing I had ever known—or so I reasoned. "Is this what is meant by debauchery?" I asked my happy friend whose pale skin bore the marks of my teeth. She only smiled. Her hair was stringy from perspiration, like a little girl who's played too long out in the heat. Pleasure-giving Claire.

Alas, what has happened to me is like nothing anyone has ever known: beyond understanding, beyond compassion, beyond comedy, though there are those, I know, who claim to be on the brink of some conclusive scientific explanation; and those, my faithful visitors, whose compassion is deeply felt, sorrowful and kind; and there are still others—there would have to be—out in the world who cannot help but laugh. And I, at times, am one with them: I understand, I have compassion, I see the joke. If only I could sustain the laughter for more than a few seconds, however—if only it wasn't so brief and so bitter. But maybe that is what I have to look forward to, if the medical men are able to sustain life in me in this condition, and if I should continue to want them to.

I am a breast. A phenomenon that has been variously described to me as "a massive hormonal influx," "an endocrinopathic catastrophe," and/or "a hermaphroditic explosion of chromosomes" took place within my body between midnight and four A.M. on February 18, 1971, and converted me into a mammary gland disconnected from any human form, a mammary gland such as could only appear, one would have thought, in a dream or a Dali painting. They tell me that I am now an organism with the general shape of a football, or a dirigible; I am said to be of a spongy consistency, weighing in at one hundred and fifty-five pounds (formerly I was one hundred and sixty-two), and measuring, still, six feet in length. Though I continue to retain, in damaged and "irregular" form, much of the cardiovascular and central nervous systems, an excretory system described as "reduced and primitive" —tubes now help me to void—and a respiratory system that terminates just above my midsection in something resembling a navel with a flap, the basic architecture in which these human characteristics are disarranged and buried is that of the breast of the mammalian female.

The bulk of my weight is fatty tissue. At one of my ends I am rounded off like a watermelon; at the other I terminate in a nipple, cylindrical in shape, projecting five inches from my "body," and perforated at the tip with seventeen openings, each about half the size of the male urethral orifice. I am told that these are the apertures of the lactiferous ducts. As I am able to understand it without the benefit of diagrams—I am sightless—the ducts branch back into lobules composed of cells of the sort that secrete the milk that is carried to the surface of the ordinary nipple when it is being suckled, or milked by mechanical means.

My flesh is smooth and "youthful" and I am still a "Caucasian," they say. My nipple is rosy pink in color. This last is thought to be unusual in that in my former incarnation I was an emphatic brunette. As I told the endocrinologist who made this observation, I myself find it less "unusual" than certain other aspects of the transformation, but then I am not the endocrinologist around here. The wit was bitter, but it was wit at last, and it must have been observed and noted that I was making an "adjustment" to my new situation.

My nipple is rosy pink in color—as was the stain

I had discovered at the base of my penis upon stepping into the shower the night this all happened to me. In that the apertures in the nipple provide me with something remotely like a mouth and ears—at least I am able to make myself understood through my nipple, and, faintly, to hear what is going on around me—I myself had assumed at first that it was my head that had become my nipple. The doctors, however, hypothesize otherwise, at least as of this month. With little more evidence, I would think, to support this conjecture over any other, they now maintain that the wrinkled, roughened skin of the nipple— which, admittedly, is exquisitely sensitive to touch like no tissue on the face, including the mucous membrane of the lips—was formed out of the glans penis. So too the puckered pinkish areola that encircles the nipple and contains the muscle system that stiffens the nipple when I am aroused, is said to have meta- morphosed from the shaft of the penis under the assault (some say) of a volcanic secretion from the pituitary of "mammogenic" fluid. Two fine long red- dish hairs extend from one of the small elevations on the rim of my areola. "They must look strange. How long are they?"

"Seven inches exactly."

"My antennae." The bitterness. Then the disbelief. "Will you pull on one of them, please?"

"If you like, David, I'll pull gently."

Dr. Gordon wasn't lying. A hair on my body had

been tugged. It was a familiar sensation, and it made me want to be dead.

Of course it was days after the change had taken place before I even regained consciousness, and another week before they would tell me anything other than that I had been "very ill" with "an endocrine imbalance," and even then, I howled so wretchedly to rediscover each time I awoke that I could neither see, smell, taste, or move, that I had to be kept under heavy sedation. When my "body" was touched I did not know what to make of it. The sensation was, unexpectedly, soothing and pleasant, but of an undifferentiated kind, reminding me of water lapping over the skin more than anything else. One morning I awakened to feel something strange happening to one of my extremities. Nothing like pain, yet I screamed, "I've been burned! I was in a fire!"

"Calm down now, Mr. Kepesh," a woman said. "I'm only washing you. I'm only washing your face."

"My face? *Where* is my face! Where are my arms! My legs! Where is my mouth! What happened to me!"

Now Dr. Gordon spoke. "You're in Lenox Hill Hospital, David. You're in a private room on the seventh floor. You've been here ten days. I've been to see you every day in the morning and again at night. You are getting excellent care and continual attention. Right now you're just being washed with a sponge and some warm soapy water. That's all. Does that hurt you?"

"No," I whimpered, "but where's my face . . .?"

"Just let the nurse wash you, and we'll talk a little later in the morning, if you're up to it. You just get all the rest you can."

"What happened to me?" All I could remember of the night in my apartment was the pain and the terror: to me it had felt as though I was being fired over and over again from a cannon into a brick wall, and then stomped on by an army of boots. In actuality it was more as though I had been a man made of taffy, stretched in opposite directions by my penis and my buttocks until I was as wide as I had once been long. The doctors believe that I could not have been conscious for more than a minute or two once the "explosion" or "catastrophe" had gotten underway, but it seems to me in retrospect that I had been awake to feel every single bone in my body broken in two and then hammered or trampled into dust.

"If you'll only relax now, David, just relax—"

"How am I being fed!"

"Intravenously. You're being fed all you need."

"Where are my arms!"

"Just let the nurse wash you, and then she'll rub some oil on you, and you'll feel much better. Then you can sleep."

I was washed like this every morning, but it must have been another week or more before I was sufficiently calm to associate the sensations accompanying the washing with the pleasures of erotic stimulation. By now I had concluded that I was a quadruple amputee. I imagined that the boiler had exploded beneath the bedroom of my parlor floor apartment, and that I had been blinded and mutilated in the explosion. I sobbed almost continuously, giving no credence whatsoever to the hormonal explanations Dr. Gordon and his colleagues continued to offer for my "illness." Then one morning, depleted and numb from my days of tearless weeping, I felt myself becoming aroused. There was a mild throbbing sensation in the vicinity of what I took still to be my "face," a pleasing feeling of—of engorgement. I was being washed.

"Do you like that?" The voice was a man's! A stranger's!

"Who are you? Where am I?"

"I'm the nurse."

"Where's the other nurse?"

"It's Sunday. Take it easy, Dave, it's only Sunday."

The next morning the regular nurse returned to duty, accompanied by Dr. Gordon. Once again as my "face" was washed I began to feel the sort of sensations that accompany erotic play, but this time I permitted them to envelop me. When she began to rub me with oil, I whispered, "That feels nice."

"What?" asked Dr. Gordon.

I could now feel each of her fingers touching me; then something was moving on me in slow, easy circles. The soft palm of her hand.

"Oh, oh," I cried, as that exquisite sense of immi-

nence that precedes a perfect ejaculation pervaded my
whole being, "oh that does feel so good!" And then I
began to sob uncontrollably and had eventually to be
put to sleep.

Shortly thereafter, Dr. Gordon, accompanied by Dr.
Klinger, who had for five years been my psychoanalyst,
told me what it is I have become.

I was washed gently but thoroughly every morning
and then my nipple and areola were lubricated with
oil. Six days a week these ablutions were performed
by a woman, Miss Clark, and on Sunday by the man. It
was ten weeks more before I had sufficiently recovered
from the horror of hearing the truth about myself to
be able to relax again beneath Miss Clark's minister-
ing hands. As it turned out, I found that I could
never submit wholly to the sexual frenzy caused by
the oiling of my nipple, until Dr. Gordon had consented to leave me alone in the room with the nurse.
But then the sensations were almost more than could
be borne, deliciously "almost"—akin to what I had
experienced in those final weeks of intercourse with
Claire, but more intense, it seemed, for coming to me
in a state of complete helplessness, in utter darkness,
and from a source unknown to me, seemingly im-
mense and dedicated solely to me and my pleasure.
By now I had been belted with a soft harness into a
contraption like a hammock—my nipple at the head,
my rounded end at the foot of the sling-like affair—
and after Miss Clark had retired from my room with

the basin of warm water and the vials of oil (I imagined vials, not bottles), my writhing would cause the hammock to sway to and fro for long, glorious minutes on end. It was swaying still when my nipple softened and I drifted off to sleep the sleep of the sated.

I say the doctor consented to leave the room. But how would I know if anyone ever left the room? It makes most sense to conclude that actually I am under continuous observation, if not by a team of scientific observers right here with me (with me in an amphitheater perhaps?), then on closed-circuit television. Dr. Gordon assures me that I am under no more surveillance than any other "difficult case," but who or what is to prevent him from deceiving me? My father? Claire? Dr. Klinger? Who could possibly be so silly as to be watching out for my civil liberties in the midst of a calamity like this? That *is* laughable. And why should I, in this state, care one way or the other if I am not alone when I think myself alone? For all I know I may be under a soundproof glass dome on a platform in the middle of Madison Square Garden, or in Macy's window—and what difference would it make? Wherever they have put me, whoever may be looking down upon me, I am really quite as alone as anyone could ever wish to be. Probably it would be best to leave off thinking too much about my "dignity," regardless of what it meant to me back when I was a professor of literature, a lover, a son, a friend, a neighbor, a customer, a client, and a citizen.

One might think that one consequence of such a transformation would be that the victim could cease for the time being to bother himself with matters of propriety and decorum and personal pride. But, as they are intimately connected to my idea of sanity and to my self-esteem, I am actually "bothered" as I wasn't in my former life, where the social constraint practiced by and large by the educated classes provided me with genuine aesthetic and ethical satisfactions. If I had become somewhat formal, even reserved, in the world-at-large at the age of thirty-eight, I do not think I was any the less unguarded or intimate with my closest friends because of it; but now, the thought that my sexual frenzy is being carried "live" on television, the thought that when I "masturbate" I am being observed from a gallery by hundreds, is deeply disturbing and *wounding*. How petty, how "inhibited" of me in the circumstances, you may say; but then, my liberated friend, what do you know about the circumstances? So: when Dr. Gordon assures me that my "privacy" is being respected, I no longer contradict him. I say, "Thank you for your consideration." In this way I am able at least to pretend to them that I think I am alone even when I am not.

You see, it is not a matter of doing what is right or seemly; I am not concerned, I can assure you, with the etiquette of being a breast. It is rather doing what I would do if I would continue to be me. And I would, for if not me, who? what? Either I continue to be

myself, or I will go mad, and then I will surely die.
And it would seem that I do not wish to die; it surprises
me some too, but it continues to be so. I don't foresee
a miracle, some sort of retaliatory raid by my *anti-
mammogenic* hormones, if such there be (and God
only knows if there are in someone made like me),
that will restore me to my previous physical propor-
tions; I suspect it's a little late for that, and so it is
not with such hope beating eternally in the breast that
the breast continues to want to exist. Human I insist
I am, but not that human. And it isn't that I am willing
to live now because I am able, because the worst is
over; I'm not at all sure that's the case. For all my
"equilibrium" and the seeming "objectivity" that per-
mits me to narrate the history of my disaster, I sometimes think the worst is yet to come. It is this then:
having been terrified of death since I was two, I
have become entrenched in my hatred of it, have taken
a position *against* death from which I cannot retreat
just because This has happened to me. Horrible as
This is, my oldest and most heartless enemy, Extinction, still strikes me as even worse. Then, you will say,
maybe *This* is not so horrible after all. Well, reader,
you say that, if you want to. All I know is that I have
been wanting not to die for so long, that I just can't
stop doing it overnight.

That I haven't died is a matter of great interest to
medical science, as you can imagine; *that* miracle
continues to be studied, I am told, by microbiologists,

physiologists, biochemists, etc., all of them working in "teams" here in the hospital and in medical institutions around the country; they are trying to figure out why I keep ticking. Dr. Klinger thinks that no matter how they put the puzzle together, in the end it may all come down to those old pulpit bromides, "strength of character" and "the will to live." So says my latter-day minister, and who am I not to concur in such a heroic estimate of myself?

"It would appear," I tell Dr. Klinger, "that my analysis has 'taken'; a tribute to you, sir." He chuckles. "You were always stronger than you thought." "I would as soon never have had to find out. And besides, it's not so. I can't live like this any longer." "Yet you have, you do." "I do *but I can't*. I was never 'strong.' Only determined. One foot in front of the other. Punctuality. Honesty. Courtesy. Good grades in all subjects. It goes back to handing my homework in on time and carrying off the prizes. Dr. Klinger, *it's hideous in here*. I want to quit, I want to go crazy, to go spinning off, ranting and wild, *but I can't*. I sob. I scream. I touch bottom. I lay there on that bottom! But then I come around. I make jokes, a little bitter and quite lame. I listen to the radio. I listen to the phonograph. I think about what we've said. I restrain my rage and restrain my rage and I wait for you to come again. But this is madness, this coming around. To be putting one foot in front of the other is madness *in that I have no feet!* A ghastly catastrophe has befallen me and I listen to the six o'clock news! I listen to the weather!" No, no, says Dr. Klinger: strength of character, the will to live.

For all that I announce at intervals that I want to go mad, it is apparently impossible: beyond me, *beneath* me. It took This for me to learn that I am a citadel of sanity.

So, though I pretend otherwise, I know they are studying me, watching me as they would watch from a glass-bottomed boat the private life of the porpoise or the whale. I think of these aquatic mammals because of the over-all resemblance I now bear to them in size and shape, and because the porpoise in particular is said to be an intelligent, perhaps even a rational, creature. I am a kind of porpoise, I tell myself, for whatever profound or whimsical reason. A beached whale. Jonah *in* the whale. "Fish out of water will do" —one of those jokes I am unable to suppress . . . In the midst of the incredible, the irredeemably ordinary appears to remind me of the level at which most of one's life is usually lived. Really, it is the silliness, the triviality, the *meaninglessness* of experience that one misses most in a state like this; for aside from the monstrous physical fact, there is of course the intellectual responsibility I seem to have developed to the uniqueness and enormity of my misfortune. WHAT DOES IT MEAN? HOW HAS IT COME TO PASS? AND WHY? IN THE ENTIRE HISTORY OF THE HUMAN RACE, WHY DAVID ALAN KEPESH? It is a

measure of Dr. Klinger's skill, I think, that he speaks
to me of "strength of character" and "the will to live,"
or as I refer to them in our meetings, s. of c., and
the w. to l. These banal phrases are the therapeutic
equivalent of my lame jokes. In these, my preposterous
times, we must keep to what is ordinary and familiar;
better the banal than the apocalyptic—for after all is
said and done, citadel of sanity though I may be, we
both recognize that there is just so much even I can
take.

As far as I know, my only visitors other than scientists, doctors, and hospital staff have been Claire, my father, and Arthur Schonbrunn, formerly my department chairman and now the Dean of the College. My father's bravery has been staggering. I do not know how to account for it, except to say that I simply never knew the man. *Nobody* knew the man. Hardworking, cunning, even tyrannical—this I did know from observing him all those years at his work; with us, his little family, he had been short-tempered, demanding, innocent, protective, tender, and deeply in love. But this self-possession in the face of horror, this composure in the face of the monstrous, who could have expected such a response from one whose life had been given over to running a second-class hotel in South Fallsburg, New York? A short order cook to begin with, he rose eventually to be the innkeeper himself; now retired, he "kills time" answering the phone mornings at his brother's booming catering service in Bayside. He comes to visit me once a week and, seated in a chair that is drawn up close to my nipple, he recounts the current adventures of people who were our guests when I was a boy. Remember Abrams the milliner? Remember Cohen the chiropodist? Remember Rosenheim with the card tricks and the Cadillac? Yes, yes, yes, I think so. Well, this one is dying, this one has moved to California, this one has a son who has married an Egyptian. "How do you like that?" he says, "I didn't even know they would allow that over there." Oh, Dad, I think to say, wonders never cease . . . But I would not dream of making such a stupid crack to him: his performance is too awesome for that. Only *is* it a performance? I think: "This is my father who used to m.c. in the casino at night—all the solemnity with which he used to introduce those waiters singing *"Eli, Eli."* This is Abe Kepesh of Kepesh's Hungarian Royale South Fallsburg. What am I to make of this? Is he a god or is he a simpleton, or is he just numb? Or is there no choice for him but to talk to me as he always has? *Doesn't he get it? Doesn't he get what has happened?*

Then he leaves—without kissing me. Something new for my father and me. And that is when I realize all that this has cost him; that is when I realize that it *is* a performance, and that my father is a great and noble man.

And my excitable mother? Mercifully for her she is

dead; if she wasn't, this would have killed her. Or would it? How noble was *she*, that chambermaid and cook? She, who put up with alcoholic bakers and homicidal salad men and bus boys who still wet the bed, could she have put up with this too? *Beasts*, she called them, *barnyard animals*, but always she went back to the kettles, back to the mops and the linens, despite the *angst* she must endure from Memorial Day weekend to Yom Kippur because of the radical human imperfection of our help. Isn't it from my mother that I inherited my determination to begin with? Isn't it to her example that I owe my survival? *There's* more banality for you: I am able to bear my transformation into a mammary gland because of my upbringing in a typically crisis-ridden Catskill hotel.

Claire, whose imperturbability has from the first been such a tonic to me, a soothing antidote to my former wife, and I suppose even to my mother and those tantrums of hers I had witnessed back in the caves of boyhood, was not as able as my father had been at neutralizing her anguish right off. What astonished me weren't her tears, however, but the weight of her head on my midsection when, five minutes or so into her first visit, she broke down and began to sob. *How can she want to touch me? How can she put her face to me?* I had been expecting that I would never be handled again by anyone other than a doctor or a nurse or a medical technician. I thought: "If Claire had turned into an enormous

27

penis . . ." But I could not see the sense of following the fantasy through to the end. What had happened to me had happened to me and no one else because it could not happen to anyone else, and even if I did not know why that was so, *it was so,* and there must be reasons to make it so, whether I was ever to know them or not. As Dr. Klinger observed in his determinedly homely style, perhaps putting myself in Claire's shoes was somewhat beyond the call of duty. Fair enough; it had seemed pointless even to me, which was why I gave up on imagining Claire Ovington as a five-foot-nine-inch male member . . . Nonetheless, I have not been able to free myself completely from feelings of shame at the thought that I could never have been capable of the devotion demonstrated by this cool, unexpansive, and notably undemonstrative young woman, neither of her devotion nor her spontaneous human sympathy.

No, not even *in extremis* have I been able to leave off determining my worth by comparison to others and admonishing myself for what I take to be deficiencies of understanding, emotion, and moral perspicacity. Admittedly, such relentless and morbid self-criticism often enough goes hand in hand with narrow self-righteousness and ingrained notions of superiority, and I wouldn't deny that in my former life I rarely had so low an opinion of myself that it was not held nicely in check by a decent regard for my virtues and qualities. All I am saying is that despite *my* alteration, my mode of apprehending and valuing myself has not been appreciably altered; and if that has been the means by which I continue to maintain my identity and my sanity and with it the w. to l., it has also in the sexual domain occasioned considerable inner turbulence and very nearly brought about my breakdown and demise.

I am speaking here of the favors I have asked of Claire, and which she grants me without complaint. After her first visit it was only a matter of days before I asked her to massage my nipple, only not "inadvertently," not chastely as the nurse did in the morning when she behaved as though she were preparing the patient for his day, rather than driving him crazy with her hands. Had Claire never laid her face upon me that first time, I doubt that I would have been so quick to make the suggestion; I might never have made it at all. But to speak frankly, the instant I felt the weight of her head upon me, heard her sobbing for me in my misery, *all* the possibilities opened up in my mind, and it was only a matter of time (and not very much of that) before I came to want from her the ultimate act of sexual grotesquerie, in the circumstances.

I should make it clear before going further that Claire is neither the Vixen nor the Virgin in spirit; throughout our affair she had been wonderfully aroused by ordinary sexual practices, robust and willing always, yet decidedly indifferent to what she seemed to think of as unessential extras. This may appear an odd statistic, since one would imagine the reverse to be the case, but she is the only woman I have known for any length of time to refuse to have intercourse *per anum*. Somewhat more to my surprise, she was from the start squeamish about receiving my sperm in her mouth, with the result that finally she came to perform fellatio only as a kind of playful antecedent to intercourse, and never as a sustained means of bringing me off, though she herself found deep orgasmic pleasure when I performed cunnilingus upon her. I did not complain bitterly about this, but from time to time, as men who have not yet been turned into breasts are wont to do, I complained—I was not, you see, getting all I wanted out of life. Otherwise, as I explained earlier, our passion during the first two years of the affair wasn't simply richer than what I'd known before, but invigorating in a charmingly new way; and even when my desire for her was markedly on the wane, it always pleased me to look at her unclothed, and I still liked to lie in bed and watch her dress in the morning and undress at night.

Actually it was Claire herself who suggested that she would play with my nipple if I wanted her to. This occurred during her fourth visit in four days; I had just described to her for the first time the strange sensual delight I experienced when I was ministered to by the nurse in the morning. My plan was to say this and no more, for the time being anyway.

But Claire said, "Would you like me to do what she does?"

"Would you—do it?"

"If you want me to, of course."

Of course. What coolness.

"I do!" I cried. "I do!"

"You tell me what you like then," she said. "You tell me what feels best."

"Is anyone in the room?"

"Just you and me."

"Is this being televised, Claire?"

"Oh no, sweetheart, no, no."

"Oh, squeeze me, squeeze me very hard!"

Once again, days later, after I made incoherent conversation for nearly an hour, Claire said, "David dearest, what is it you want? Do you want me to put my mouth on it?"

"Yes! Yes!"

How could she? How can she? Why does she? Would *I*? I say to Dr. Klinger, "It's too much to ask. It's too awful. I have to stop this. I want her to do it all the time, every minute she's here. I don't want her to read to me—I don't even listen. I don't even want to talk any more. I just want her to squeeze me and suck me and lick me. I can't get enough of it. I can't stand when she stops. I shout, I scream, 'Go on! Go on!' I can't stand when she leaves, because I want *more*. But I'll drive her away. I have to stop. It *will* drive her away finally. Then I'll have no one. Then

I'll have just the nurse in the morning and that will be that. My father will come and tell me who died and who got married. And you will come and tell me about my strong character, *but I won't have a woman.* I won't have love and sex ever again! I can imagine Claire, I can envision her—I see her sucking on me! I want her to take her clothes off—but I'm afraid to ask her! I don't want to drive her away—it's bizarre enough as it is, but still I can imagine she has her clothes off, I want them off, at her feet, on the floor. I want her to get up on me, and *roll* on me. Oh, Doctor, you know what I really want? I want to fuck her! I want that big girl to bend over at the head of the hammock and stick my nipple in her cunt from behind. And move on it, up and down—I want her to go mad on my nipple! But I'm afraid if I even say it it will drive her away! That she'll run and never return!"

Claire visits in the evening, after her dinner, and on weekends. During the day she teaches fourth grade at the Bank Street School here in New York. She is a Phi Beta Kappa graduate of Cornell; her mother is principal of a school in Schenectady, divorced now from her father, an engineer with Western Electric; her older sister, the more conservative of the two Ovington daughters, is married to an economist in the Commerce Department, and lives with him and four tow-headed children in Alexandria, Virginia. They own a house on the South Beach of Martha's Vineyard where Claire and I visited them on our way to a week's vacation in Nantucket last summer. We argued politics—the war. That done, we played fly-catcher-up with the kids down on the beach and then went off to eat boiled lobsters in Edgartown; afterward, we sat in the movies, wind-burned faces and buttered fingers. Delicious. We had a fine time, really, "square" as our hosts were; I know they were "square" because they kept telling me they were. Yet we had such a good time. Claire, a green-eyed blonde, is lean and very long-legged but full in the breast. "Imagine how they'll hang at fifty," she says, "if they hang like this at twenty-five." "Can't," I say, and in the hollow of the dunes, having unclipped the top of her bikini and watched it drop away, I stretch on my back in the hot sand, dig down with my heels, close my eyes, open my lips, and wait for her to lower a breast all the way into my mouth. What a sensation, there with the sea booming below! As though it were the globe itself— soft globe!—and I some Poseidon or Zeus! No wonder the Greeks imagined anthropomorphic gods—those are the only gods who have fun. "Let's spend all next summer by the ocean," say I, as people do on the first day of a vacation. "First let's go home and make love," whispers tall, bare-breasted Claire, kneeling beside me; she imagines I am aroused, as of old. "Oh, let's just lie here. Hey, where is that thing? Back in my mouth, Miss." "I don't want to cut off your air. You were turning green." "With envy," I say.

Yes, that I said. I admit openly that I said it. And if this were a fairy tale we would now understand the moral: "Beware fanciful desires; you may get lucky." But this is a true story, if not for you, reader, for me. I have wanted to be many things in my life far less whimsically than I wanted on that beach to be breasted, or Claire's breast. If this *is* a fairy tale, why is it that that innocent wish (if "wish" it even was) made to charm and to flatter rather than to come true, flowing not out of yearning but out of happiness and high spirits, why was that wish granted to me, while hopes and dreams of far greater urgency, voiced stridently, repeatedly, and in despair, only came to be realized by putting one foot in front of the other in front of the other in front of the other in front of the other . . . No, the victim does not subscribe to the wish-fulfillment theory, and I advise you not to, neat and fashionable and delightfully punitive as it may be. Reality is grander than that. Reality has more style. There. For those of you who cannot live without one, a moral to this tale. "Reality has style," concludes the embittered professor who became a female breast. Go, you sleek, self-satisfied Houyhnhnms, and moralize on that!

It was not to Claire that I made the "ultimate" proposal, then, but to my female nurse. I said, "Do you know what I think about when you wash me like this? Can I tell you what I am thinking about right now?"

"What is that, Mr. Kepesh?"

"I would like to fuck you with my nipple, Miss Clark."

"I can't hear you, Mr. Kepesh."

"I get so excited I want to fuck you! I want you to sit on my nipple—with your cunt!"

Without taking so much as a second to consider her words (training will out), she said, "I'll be finished now in just a moment, Mr. Kepesh."

I cry, writhing, *Did you hear me, you whore!*

"Now we'll be finished here in just a moment . . ."

By the time Dr. Klinger arrived at four I was one hundred and fifty-five pounds of shame and remorse. The aftereffects of losing control were worse than I had expected. I even began to sob a little when I told Dr. Klinger what I had gone ahead and done, against all my misgivings and despite his words of warning. *Now*, I said, it was recorded on tape; it had been observed by the hundreds (or thousands) staring down at me from the gallery—or the bleachers. For all I knew it would be on page one of tomorrow morning's tabloids. What a laugh it would provide for the straphangers! For there was, of course, a humorous side to it: what is a catastrophe, without its humorous side? Miss Clark, you see, is a spinster, fifty-six years old and, I am told, on the short and stocky side. And I had known this all along.

Unlike Dr. Gordon and Claire and my father, who assure me continually that I am not being watched other than by those who announce their presence, Dr.

35

Klinger has never really bothered to dispute me on this issue. "And?" he said. "If it is on page one? What of it?"

"It's nobody's business!"

"But you would like to do it, wouldn't you?"

"Yes! Yes! But she ignored me! She pretended I'd asked her to hurry up and be done! I don't want her any more! I can't stand that efficient bitch! I want a new nurse!"

"Who do you have in mind?"

"Someone young—and beautiful! Why not!"

"And who will say yes?"

"Yes! Yes! Why not! Why shouldn't I have that if I want it! It's insane otherwise! I should be allowed to have it all day long! This is no longer ordinary life and I am not going to pretend that it is! *You* want me to be *ordinary*—*you* expect me to be *ordinary* in this condition! I'm supposed to be a sensible man—when I am like this! But that's crazy on your part, Doctor! I want her to sit on me with her cunt! Why not! I want Claire to! *Why won't Claire do it!* She'll do everything else! Why won't she do that! Why is *that* too grotesque! What do any of you know about grotesque! What is more grotesque anyway, but to be denied my little pleasure in the midst of this relentless nightmare! Why shouldn't I be rubbed and oiled and massaged and sucked and licked and fucked, too, if I want it! Why shouldn't I have anything and everything I can think of *every single minute of the day* if that can transport me from this miserable hell! Tell me why that shouldn't be! Instead you torture me! Instead you prevent me from having what I want! Instead I lie here being sensible! There's the madness, Doctor, *being sensible!*"

I do not know how much of what I said Dr. Klinger even understood; it is apparently difficult enough to make out my words when I am speaking loud and clear, and now I was sobbing and howling with no regard for the camera or the spectators in the stands . . . Or was that *why* I was carrying on so? Was I really so racked as all this by the indecent proposal I had made that morning to my nurse? Or was this hysterical episode for the benefit of my great audience out there, to convince them that I am still a man— for who but a man has conscience, reason, desire, and remorse?

This crisis lasted for several months. I became increasingly lewd with the stout and dutiful Miss Clark, graphic, abusive, craven—finally, one morning during my washing, spinning in my ecstasy like a top, I offered her money, as much as she wanted, to pull down her girdle and stick my nipple up into her cunt. "Bend over—take it from behind! I'll give you anything you want!" How I would get the money from my account into her hands, how I would go about borrowing if she wanted more than I had, was something I tried to figure out during the long, lonely day. Because I knew there was no one really to assist me, I was never

D

able to complete the transaction other than in a haze of magical masturbatory possibilities . . . At this time, though some five months into my new existence, I was still unwilling to be visited by anyone but Claire and my father, still far too vulnerable. Now this may seem ridiculous, given how strongly I believed that my activities were being recorded on tape and publicized in the *Daily News*. But I am not arguing here that I have been able to conquer altogether the most blatantly contradictory feelings, or to squelch, without a struggle, spasms of illogic or infantilism. I am only describing how I have come to reach my present state of melancholy equilibrium . . . Of course, to aid me, I could easily have called upon a friend, a young bearded colleague in the English Department at Stony Brook, a clever poet from Brooklyn; he could have gotten hold of the money for me, and made the necessary financial arrangements in my behalf, either with Miss Clark, or if she continued to be bound by professional ethics, with some woman whose profession might permit her to satisfy this desire of mine for a price. My young colleague was not a prude and he liked adventure. But then neither was I a prude, and once upon a time I had had a taste for adventure certainly no less developed than his own was in the sexual line. Regardless of how I may have expressed my confusion in the midst of ranting at Dr. Klinger, you must understand that at bottom it was not a sense of sexual wrongdoing that made me the victim of wildly polar feelings about my desire. I had, easily enough, experimented with a dozen or so whores back in my early twenties, and during a year as a Fulbright student in London, I had for several months carried on a strange, over-wrought affair with two young women, students my age on leave together from the University of Lund in Sweden, who shared a basement and a bed in Blooms-bury with me, until the less stable beauty of the two halfheartedly tried to pitch herself under a lorry in Camden High Street. It was not then a man of exceed-ingly narrow experience and painful inhibitions who was being so tormented; what alarmed me so about giving in to this grotesque yearning was that by so doing I might be severing myself irreparably from my own past and my own kind. I was afraid that if I were to become habituated to such practices, my appetites could only become progressively strange, until at last I reached a peak of disorientation from which I would fall—or leap—into the void. I would go mad. I would cease to know who I had been or what I was. I would cease to know anything. And even if I should not die as a result, what would I have become but a lump of flesh and no more?

So, with Dr. Klinger's assistance, I undertook to try to extinguish, and if not to extinguish, at least (in the doctor's favorite word) to *tolerate* the desire to insert my nipple into somebody's vagina. But with all my will power—and that can be considerable when I marshal my forces—I was simply out of my depth once the washing got underway; and so in the end it was decided that in order to assist me in my heroic undertaking, my nipple and areola would be sprayed with a mild anesthetizing solution before Miss Clark started in preparing me for my day. And though the chilling spray didn't completely block out all sensation, it so reduced it as to give me the upper hand in the battle —a battle which I finally won, however, only when the doctors decided, with my consent, to change my nurse from a woman to a man.

That did the trick. For even back before the spray, I was never able to sweep aside the homosexual taboo and imagine my nipple, for instance, in the mouth or the anus of Mr. Brooks, the male nurse, though I realize that the conjunction of male mouth and female nipple can hardly be described as a homosexual act. Still, on Sundays, when he was the one to wash and oil me, though I could never restrain my writhing, my dreams—my screams—were for Miss Clark or Claire or that call girl whom we would pay in handfuls of hundreds for spreading back the lips of her vagina and wiggling down over the length of my erect nipple with her hired parts . . . At any rate, to conclude this chapter on a note of triumph, I am able now—temporarily anesthetized and in the hands of a man—to receive my morning ablutions like any other invalid, more or less.

And there is still Claire—angelic Claire!—to "make

love" to me, if not with her vagina, with her fingers and her mouth. And isn't that sufficient? My God— isn't that incredible enough? Of course I always want MORE, would die for MORE (or lack of it), for there is no orgasmic finale to my excitement, no explosion and release, only the sustained sense of imminent ejaculation in which I writhe from the first second to the last. But as it happens, I have actually come to settle for less rather than MORE. Only for half of her hour-long visits do I ask Claire to attend to my lust. Largely it is for the same reason that I did not ask her to have vaginal intercourse with my nipple that I have reduced the length of time given over to purely sensual delight: I do not want to lose her. I do not want her to come to see herself as some kind of machine called here to service this preposterous organism, something with whom David Kepesh has no interest in maintaining ordinary human contact of a reciprocal nature. I do not know how much longer I can depend upon her to remember who I was or what we were together, angelic, *saintly* as she has been. Surely the more time we spend in conversation, even in small talk and gossip, the greater chance I have to hold her affection and loyalty. I am even considering cutting in half yet again the time given over to the stimulation of my nipple. I reason this way: if the excitement is always at the same sexual pitch, neither increasing or decreasing in intensity once it is under way, what is the difference if I experience it for fifteen rather than thirty minutes? What is the difference if I experience it for only *one* minute?

Mind you, I am not yet equal to such renunciation, nor am I convinced that it is desirable even from Claire's point of view. But it is something, I tell you, for me even to *entertain* such an idea after the torment of desire I have known. Even now there are still moments, infrequent but searing, when I have all I can do not to cry out to the beautiful young fourth-grade teacher and Phi Beta Kappa graduate of Cornell University whose lips are tight over the seventeen apertures of my nipple, "Fuck on it, Ovington! Fuck on it with your cunt!" But I don't, I don't. If Claire was of a mind to go that far with me, she would have made the suggestion herself long ago. Not only am I attuned to the meaning of her silence, but I am determined not to cause her to consider too carefully the grotesqueries in which she has already, miraculously, declared herself willing to participate.

Sometime between the first and the second of the two major "crises" I have survived so far here in the hospital—if hospital it is—I was visited by Arthur Schonbrunn. He is the Dean of the College of Arts and Sciences at Stony Brook, and an acquaintance from my school days at Palo Alto, back when he was *the* young hot-shot professor and I was a graduate student getting a Ph.D. It was Arthur—as chairman of a newly formed comparative literature department here—who brought me to Stony Brook from Stanford eight years ago. Now he is nearly fifty, a wry, articulate man, and for an academic uncommonly, almost alarmingly, suave in manner and dress. To this day he is something of a puzzle to me, more than ever a puzzle, I should say, since that visit he paid nine months ago.

Schonbrunn is one of those academics (often enough deans and provosts, occasionally just drunks)

who produce a work of intellectual distinction in their
early thirties—in his case, a sharp little book on the
fiction of Robert Musil, at that time a novelist largely
untranslated and all but unknown to American readers
—and then are never heard from again; the second
book (Arthur's was to have been on Heinrich von
Kleist), the one they are writing summers and weekends and plan to finish "on sabbatical," is alluded to
for about a decade, until at last the author has risen
so high in university circles that it is impossible to
imagine he has an existence outside of the committee
room, let alone a typewriter in his attic at which he
sits in solitude on a Saturday, or late at night, to
ponder anything as irreducible as the fictions of a
Kleist. Probably Arthur will be our president one day
—of Stony Brook first, then, if his wife has her way,
of the United States of America. Some say that Debbie
Schonbrunn is the Lady Macbeth of Long Island, which
is saying something, since Long Island stretches quite
a ways out to sea. That she has airs enough to fill the
sails of all the schooners ever anchored in the Sound,
and the ambition to go with it, is not something I
would care to dispute; but then Dean Schonbrunn is
no milquetoast and no fool, and I, for one, had never
been able to believe that it was to his wife's Kennedy-
esque dreams, rather than his own, that he had sac-
rificed his belletristic gift. His confidence with men,
his power over an audience of two or two thousand,
his spectacularly suave and diplomatic ways—all this

well-oiled machinery of his had always put me off some, but nonetheless it encouraged the belief that here was a man more or less his own master. But then he came to visit me nine months ago—wrote a beautifully tactful note beforehand, asking if he might—and utterly astounded me (and nearly destroyed me) by his unspeakable behavior. I have since concluded that it was hardly the behavior of a man at one with his desires. I have had to conclude something, you see, and that is it.

Arthur came here in both his official and unofficial capacities. I chose him to be my first visitor from among all my colleagues (and as it has turned out, my last), precisely because his strong sense of role, in conjunction with our longstanding acquaintanceship, led me (and Dr. Klinger) to think that he would be someone whose presence I could "manage," a good reliable person with whom to make my social debut following my victory over rampaging lust. In his own smooth way, Arthur had been generous and considerate of me always—I am still considered something of his "protégé"—and then too there was his renowned self-possession to assure us that he would not be benumbed or horrified, or, what was worse, unduly plaintive or consoling. I also had the idea that if not during this visit, then on the next, or the next after that, I would propose to Arthur a way in which I might be able to maintain my professional affiliation with the university. Back at Stanford I had been a "reader" for one of the enormous sophomore classes that he lectured in "Masterpieces of Western Literature"—couldn't I perform some such secondary function again? Claire would read student papers aloud to me, and I could dictate to her corrections, comments, and grades . . . Or was such an arrangement simply out of the question? With Arthur Schonbrunn, we thought, there would be no harm at least in asking.

I never even got the chance. Even while I was thanking him for the thoughtful note he had sent, even as I was telling him, a little "tearfully"—I couldn't help myself—how touched I was that he should come to see me and talk with me, I thought I could hear giggling. "Arthur," I asked, "are we alone—?"

He said, "Yes." Then giggled, quite distinctly! Sightless, I could still picture my former mentor: in his blue blazer with the paisley lining made in London by Kilgore, French, who had clothed Jack Kennedy before him—in his soft flannel trousers and gleaming Gucci loafers, the diplomatic Dean of the College of Arts and Sciences, soon to be Secretary-General of the U.N. at the very least—giggling! Wearing his not-too-kempt, not-too-unkempt mop of impressive salt-and-pepper hair, the bastard had begun to laugh! And I hadn't even made my suggestion yet about becoming a reader for the department; he was laughing not because of anything ludicrous I had proposed, but because he saw that it was true, I actually *had* turned into a breast. My graduate school mentor, my superior, the most courtly gentleman I had ever known, was, from the sound of it, overcome by hilarity *simply at the sight of me!*

"I'm—I'm—David, I'm sorry that I—I'm—I—" But now he was howling so, he couldn't even speak coherently. *Arthur Schonbrunn unable to speak coherently.* Talk about the incredible. Twenty, thirty seconds of howling, and then he was gone. In all, the visit had lasted about two minutes.

Two days later came the apology, as elegantly done, I'd say, as anything Arthur's turned out since the little book on Musil. And the following week, to the day—what a talent for timing those climbers have— the package from Sam Goody's, with the little card signed Debbie and Arthur S., written in Debbie's hand, Claire tells me, and more than likely her very own idea.

An LP recording of the Laurence Olivier version of *Hamlet*. Shakespeare, William. Oh perfect! Thou restoreth my soul, Deborah, *and* yours *and* the Dean's, all with one tastefully chosen LP! Shakespeare! Pretentious philistine bitch! Where's my set of Balzac in deluxe leather bindings! Where's my membership in the Great Books Club! Why not Beethoven's Fifth, you Jacqueline-*manqué!*

Arthur had written: "Your misfortune should not have had to be compounded by a feeble man such as myself. I'm at a loss to explain what came over

47

me. It would strike us both as so much cant if I even tried." On the fortieth or fiftieth time round, I finally came up with this response that I dictated to Claire and which she mailed for me. "Dear Debbie and Arthur S. Thanx mucho for the groovy sides. Dave 'The Breast' K." I checked twice with Claire to be sure she had spelled thanks with that x before she went ahead and sealed the envelope . . The notes previously dictated, but discarded, had been gracious, eloquent, forgiving, light-hearted, grave, hangdog, literary, noncommittal, businesslike, arch, angry, vehement, vicious, wild, snide, dadaesque—some had even been sillier than the one I sent. Why I told Claire to post that one rather than any of the others isn't worth considering; whatever I wrote those two meant nothing, just as *whatever* Arthur had done here that afternoon he visited would have meant nothing. It is a measure of Claire's good sense, and her grasp of the issue here, that she mailed it (if she mailed it) without making any objection to the content or the tone; she knew it meant nothing too.

"Feeble?" I wrote Arthur, in the very first note I'd asked Claire to take down, virtually seconds after she'd read me his, "Why, if anything it is evidence of your earthy vitality that you should have laughed so hard. I am the feeble one, otherwise I would have joined in. I fail to appreciate the enormous comedy of all this only because I am really more of an Arthur Schonbrunn than you are, you vain, narcissistic, dandified prick!" But am I? Is that the fundamental truth here, reader? Is it my vanity that hurts most of all? Is that all my "dignity" really was—and is? Oh, for a good deep belly laugh then, at my own expense! A laugh starting way down at my watermelon end and swelling till it joyously trickles forth from the apertures in my nipple.

The second crisis that threatened to undo me, and that for the time being (I must make that qualification continually) I appear to have weathered, might be called my crisis of faith. As it came fully a month after Arthur's visit, it is hard to say for sure whether it was precipitated in any way by that bizarre little event; I am long since over hating Arthur Schonbrunn for wounding me so that day—at least I am working at being long since over it—and so presently I tend to agree with Dr. Klinger that though Arthur's visit may have speeded things up, what I had to struggle through next was more or less inevitable.

What happened was this: I refused to believe that I had turned into a breast. Having with great effort brought my fantasies of intercourse almost completely under control, I was overcome with the realization that all this was impossible. A man cannot turn into a breast other than in his own imagination. The shock of it all had been so enormous that it had taken me nearly six months to question the reality of it. "But, look, this isn't happening—it can't!"

"Why can't it?" asked Dr. Klinger.

"You know why! Any child knows why! Because it is a physiological and biological and anatomical impossibility, that's why!"

"How then do you explain your predicament?"

"It's a dream! This is all some sort of dream! Six months haven't passed—that's an illusion! I'm dreaming! It's just a matter of waking up!"

"But you are awake, Mr. Kepesh. You know that you're awake."

"Stop saying that! Don't torture me like that! Let me get up! Enough! I want to wake up!"

For days—or, I decided, what pass for days in a nightmare—I struggled to awaken. Claire came, my father came, my nurse Mr. Brooks came—some mornings he patted me just at the edge of my areola to rouse me. In the first seconds of consciousness I imagined that I was wide awake and a breast, only to realize in horror that I had not been awakened from a real sleep, but from the sleep that I slept within the nightmare itself, and that I was still David Alan Kepesh, dreaming. This is a dream! Stop torturing me! *Let me get up!* I howled and cursed at my captors, though of course if it was a dream I was only cursing captors of my own invention. Still I cursed: Claire, you cold-hearted cunt! Father, you ignoramus! Mr. Brooks, you sadistic fag! Klinger, you liar! Gordon, you know-nothing! I cursed the spectators in the gallery that I had constructed, I cursed the television technicians on the television circuit I had imagined—voyeurs! heartless voyeurs!—and on and on, until at last, fearing that my damaged system could not stand up to such a sustained psychic assault (yes, those were the words I put into their clever mouths), they decided to place me under heavy sedation. How I howled then! "Thugs!" I cried. "Criminals! Fiends!" even as I sank beneath the numbing effect of the drug, and they dragged me, thrashing and screaming, from my black cell down to a dungeon blacker still, to utter isolation and heavy, heavy chains.

When I came around I understood for the first time that I had gone mad. I was not dreaming, I was crazy. There was to be no magical "waking up," no throwing off this nightmare to get up out of bed, to brush my teeth, to drive out on the expressway to Long Island to teach; if there was to be anything (and I prayed that there was and that I was not *so* far gone), it was the long road back, getting better, becoming sane again. And of course the first big step toward recovering my sanity was this realization that my sense of myself as a breast, my life as a breast, was the delusion of a lunatic.

Now I did not understand at all how it was I had come to lose my sanity or why. Remembering what it was that had precipitated so complete a schizophrenic collapse was beyond me, but then that wasn't an argument against my new hypothesis, for whatever could have produced my breakdown would inevitably have been so frightening that I would have *had* to obliterate all memory of it. Couldn't it be that I was actually sitting in a room in a mental institution at this very moment, locked in this profound delusional condition? That I could not see, that I could not taste, that I could not smell, that I could only faintly hear, that I could not make contact with my own anatomy, that I experienced myself as speaking to others like one buried in, and very nearly strangulated by, his own adipose tissue—were these symptoms so unfamiliar in the netherworld of psychosis?

But, I reasoned, if all this is so, why then is Dr. Klinger—and that it was Dr. Klinger, I was sure; I had after all to be sure of something if I was to make a start, so I clung to his mildly accented English, his straightforward manner, his homely humor, as proof that at least *this* in my experience was real—why then is Dr. Klinger telling me that my sanity depends upon my *accepting* my condition, that my sanity depends upon learning how to maintain my equilibrium despite this horrendous accident, when in fact the way back to health is clearly to *challenge,* to *defy,* this preposterous conception of myself? The answer was obvious: that wasn't at all what Dr. Klinger was saying. In the service of my disease I was taking his words, simple and clear as they undoubtedly were, and giving them precisely the opposite meaning from that which he intended for them.

When he came for my session that afternoon, I

called forth all of my famous determination in order to explain to him as simple and clearly as *I* was able, the discovery I had made that morning. I wept with joyous relief when I was finished, but otherwise I was as inspired in speech as I have ever been. Sometimes in teaching one hears oneself speaking in perfect cadences, with just the right emphasis and timing, developing ideas into rounded sentences and combining them in paragraphs full to brimming, and it is hard then to believe that the fellow now addressing his hushed students with a golden tongue and great decisiveness was confusing them just the hour before with the most unconvincing literary speculation delivered forth in rags and tatters. Imagine then how hard it was for me to associate the measured voice now addressing Dr. Klinger with the howling of the madman I had been prior to my week under sedation. If I was still a lunatic—and still a breast, I was still a lunatic—I was undoubtedly one of the more lucid and eloquent ones on my floor.

I said, "Curiously, it's Arthur Schonbrunn's visit that makes me certain I'm on the right track at last. How could I ever have believed that Arthur would come here and *laugh*? How could I ever have accepted such an utterly paranoid delusion for the truth? For a month now I've been cursing him and Debbie, and none of it makes any sense at all, because if there is one person in the world who simply would not lose control in such a situation, it's Arthur."

"He is beyond the perils of human nature, this Dean?"

"You know something? The answer to that is yes. He is beyond the perils of human nature."

"Such a shrewd operator."

"It isn't that he's so shrewd—that's going at it wrong way round. It's that I've been so mad. I made that all up. God. God!"

"And the note of his you answered so graciously? The note that made you so livid?"

"More paranoia."

"And the recording?"

"Ah, *that's* Mr. Reality. *That's* real. Right up Debbie's alley. Oh yes, I can *feel* the difference now, even as I talk, I can sense the difference between the actual and the imaginary, between the insane stuff and what's truly happened. Oh, I do feel the difference, *you must believe me*. I've gone mad, but now I know it!"

"And what do you think caused you, as you put it, 'to go mad'?" Dr. Klinger asked.

"I don't remember."

"Do you have any idea at all? What could possibly have brought someone like yourself to such a fully developed and impenetrable delusion?"

"I'm telling you the truth, Doctor. I don't have any idea. Not as yet, anyway."

"What comes to mind? Anything at all?"

"Well, what comes to mind—what came to mind

this morning—doesn't really seem sufficient or con-
vincing."

"What is it?"

"I'm grasping at straws, you see. I thought, 'I got it
from fiction.' The books I've been teaching inspired it.
They put the idea in my head. I don't mean to sound
whimsical, but I'm thinking of my European Literature course. Teaching Gogol and Kafka every year—
teaching 'The Nose' and 'Metamorphosis.' "

"Of course, many professors teach 'The Nose' and
'Metamorphosis.' "

"But maybe," I said, the humor intentional now,
"not with so much conviction as I do."

He laughed too.

"I *am* mad, though—aren't I?" I asked.

"No."

The setback was only momentary: I realized he must
have said "Yes" and I had instantaneously turned it to
its opposite, as we turn rightside up the images that
flash upon the retina upside down.

"I want to tell you that though you just answered
'Yes' when I asked whether I was mad, I heard you
say 'No.' "

"I did say no. You are not mad. You are not in the
grip of a delusion, or haven't been till now. You have
not suffered what you call 'a schizophrenic collapse.'
You are a breast, of sorts. You have been heroic in
your efforts to accommodate yourself to this mysterious misfortune. I can understand the temptation,

even the necessity at some point, to give in to the appealing idea that this is all just a dream, a hallucination, a delusion, or what have you—perhaps a drug-induced state. But it is none of these things. It is something that has happened to you. And the way *to* madness, Mr. Kepesh, do you hear me?—*the way into madness*, is to pretend otherwise. The comfort of that will be short-lived, I can assure you. I want to steer you away from this course before you go any further. I want you to disabuse yourself of the notion that you are insane. You are not insane and to pretend to be insane will only bring you to grief. Insanity is no solution, neither imagined insanity nor the real thing."

"Again I heard everything reversed. I turned the sense of your words completely around."

"No you did not."

"Let me ask you, does it make any sense to you at all to think that this particular delusion was somehow fueled by years of teaching those stories? I mean regardless of whatever the trauma was that actually triggered the whole thing."

"But there was no trauma of a psychological kind, and this, as I have told you, is no delusion."

With an irony that pleased me—and bespoke health! health!—I said, "But if it *were*, Dr. Klinger—since I just understood you to say once again that it is not a delusion—*if* it were, would you *then* be willing to see some connection between the kind of hallucination I've embedded myself in, and the power over my imagination of Kafka, or of Gogol? Or of Swift? I'm thinking of *Gulliver's Travels*, which I've also been teaching for years. Dr. Klinger, do you hear *me*? Perhaps if we proceed this way, speaking of my disease as a hypothetical—"

"But to repeat yet again: there is no disease in the psychic realm. That is to say there has been none thus far. There has been shock, panic, fury, despair, disorientation, profound feelings of helplessness and isolation, deep depression, but through it all, quite miraculously, nothing I would call disease. Not even when your old friend the Dean showed up and had a laughing fit. That shocked you. It still shocks you. You were terribly crushed by that. Why wouldn't you be? And it does not help any, I know, to be told that he is a man with his own vulnerable self to deal with. It was ghastly for you to have heard such laughter, even if the laugh had less to do with you than with the precarious grip such a person has on life, beneath all the glibness and the tailor-made clothes. You didn't make up Arthur Schonbrunn's visit, Mr. Kepesh, you didn't make up what happened to him here. *It happened.* You are pretending to be a naïf, you know, when you tell me such a reaction from him, or anyone, is 'impossible.' You are a better student of human nature than that. You've read too much Dostoevsky for that."

"Shall I repeat to you what I thought I heard you say?"

"No need. What you thought you heard, you heard. Come off it, Mr. Kepesh—and the sooner the better. As you suggest yourself, this literary speculation that you make in a spirit of whimsy, Gogol, Kafka, and so on—it is going to get you into serious trouble if you keep it up. Proceed further with this line of thought and you will so weaken the hold that *you* happen to have on a uniquely difficult reality, that the next thing you know, you will have *produced* genuine and irreversible delusions exactly like those you now claim to have. Do you follow me, Mr. Kepesh? You are a highly intelligent man and you have a very strong will, and I want you to stop it right now."

It was exhausting, this imaginary combat, but then I no longer expected that getting back to where I had begun was going to be as simple as waking up from a bad dream. It was going to be hell, but what was that hell to this one?

"Dr. Klinger!" I cried. "Listen to me—I won't let it drive me crazy! Whatever it is, I won't let it drive me crazy any more! I will fight my way out of this! I swear to you, I'll fight till I'm in shreds! I will stop hearing the opposite! I will start hearing what you are all saying to me! Do you hear me, Doctor? Do you understand *my* words? I will not accept this delusion! I will not be its captive! I will not be its victim! You *will* get through to me! Don't give up on me!" I pleaded. "Do you hear me? Do you understand me? Please don't give up on me! Don't give me up for lost! I'll break through this thing and be myself again! I will!"

Now my days were given over entirely to trying to penetrate what I heard so as to get at what actually was being said to me, whether by the doctors, Mr. Brooks, or Claire. This required a kind of unfocused yet continuous effort of the will so depleting that by nightfall I felt it would take no more than a puff from a child's lips to snuff out the wavering little flame of memory and intelligence and hope that still claimed to be David Alan Kepesh.

When my father came to visit on Sunday I told him the good news, even though I was certain that Dr. Klinger and Claire must have notified him already. I babbled like a boy who'd won a trophy. I told him that it was true, I no longer believed I was a breast. If I had not yet been able to throw off the physical side of the hallucination, I was daily divesting myself of the psychic delusion; every day, every hour, I sensed myself turning back into myself, and I could even see through to the time when I would be back before my classes, teaching Gogol and Kafka rather than experiencing vicariously the unnatural transformations those writers had imagined for the characters in their famous fictions. Since my father knows nothing of books, I went on in a bubbly boyish way, telling how Gregor Samsa awakens one morning in the Kafka masterpiece to find that he has turned into an enormous beetle; I gave him a summary of 'The Nose,' recounted briefly how Gogol's hero awakens to find *himself* missing his nose, sets out looking for it in St. Petersburg, places an ad in the newspaper requesting its return, sees "it" walking on the street, et cetera, until in the end it just shows up back on his face for no better reason than it had disappeared. (I could hear him thinking, "You teach this stuff, in a college?") I explained that I still could not remember the trauma that had done me in; it had been so terrifying that even now I simply became deaf, *could not hear,* when the doctor tried to remind me of it. It was going to take time, I told him, a great deal of time, but at least I was on the way back. I had begun the journey, had placed one foot in front of the other. I explained to him that whatever the traumatic event itself had been, it appeared that in order to escape it I had grabbed hold of the handiest preposterous idea, which was the Kafkaesque, Gogolian fantasy of physical transformation that I had been talking about in my classroom only the week preceding the catastrophe. Now, with Dr. Klinger's assistance, I was trying to figure out why it was a breast that I had imagined myself to be. What whirling chaos of desire and fear had erupted in this primitive identification with *the* object of infantile veneration? What unfulfilled appetites or ancient confusions, what fragments out of my remotest past could have collided to spark a mammoth delusion of such splendid, such *classical* simplicity? How explain the "mammary envy" that might be thought to have inspired so extravagant an invention? Was I just another American boy raised on a diet too rich with centerfolds? Or was it rather a longing in me, deep down in my molten center, a churning longing to be utterly and blessedly helpless, to be a big brainless bag of tissue, desirable, dumb, passive, immobile, acted upon instead of acting, hanging, *there*, as a breast hangs and is *there*. Or think of it as a form of hibernation, a long winter's sleep buried in the mountains of the female anatomy. Or, or, think of the breast as my cocoon, first cousin to that sac in which I had trod my mother's waters. Or, or, or. I babbled, I went beyond him certainly, but then I went beyond myself, and common sense as well —but where *was* one to get a purchase on a phenomenon such as this? So I babbled to my Daddy out of my madness, and then, once again, in my joy, I wept. No tears, but I wept. Where were my tears? When would I feel tears again? When would I feel my teeth, my tongue, my toes?

For a long while my father said nothing. Perhaps, I thought, he is crying too. Then he went into the weekly news report: so-and-so's daughter is pregnant, so-and-so's son has bought a hundred-thousand-dollar house, my uncle is catering Richard Tucker's younger brother's son's wedding.

In my excitement, I now realized, I had been totally incomprehensible. Having defeated the idea that I was a breast, I had forgotten that for some reason it still required that I virtually give a recitation, as from a stage, whenever I wanted to make my every word understood. Something was still wrong with my volume control, or maybe the trouble was in my hearing apparatus, for I still tended apparently to mumble or whisper when I believed I was speaking in a normal conversational tone. But one thing I knew: it wasn't because my voice box was buried in a one-hundred-and-fifty-five-pound mammary gland. My body was still my body! I repeated, in my most booming voice, more or less what I had just told him about my breakthrough. Then I thought to say—how slowly light dawns for the insane—"Dad, where are we?"

"In your room," he answered.

"And have I turned into a breast?"

"Well, that's what they say."

"But that's not true! I'm a mental patient! Tell me again. What am I?"

"Oh, Davie."

"What am I?"

"You're a woman's breast."

"That's not true! What I heard you say is not true! I'm a mental patient! In a hospital! And you are visiting me! Dad, if that's the truth, I want you just to say yes. Listen to me now: I am a mental patient. I am in a hospital. I have had a severe breakdown. Yes or no. *Tell me the truth*."

And my father answered, "Yes, son, yes. You're a mental patient."

"I heard him!" I cried to Dr. Klinger when he came for our hour later in the day. "I heard my father! I've broken all the way through! I heard the truth! I heard him say I was a mental patient!"

"He should never have told you that."

"I heard it! It didn't get reversed!"

"Your father loves you. He's a simple man, and he loves you a great deal. He thought it would help if he said that. He knows now that it can't. And so do you know it can't."

But I was beside myself, and wept and wept. My father had gotten through to me; the others would follow soon enough. "I heard it!" I said. "I'm not a breast! I'm mad!"

In the next week I begin to make progress, at least to hear me tell it. What theories I devise to account for my delusion! How ingenious in my desperation to be cured! How I strain to be sane and whole! I dredge the muck of my beginnings in search of a single glittering memory of my hungering gums at the spigot, my nose in the nourishing globe. "If she were alive, if she could tell me—!" "Tell you what?" asks Dr. Klinger. I moan. How do I know? But where else to begin but there—only there there is nothing. It is all too far back, back where I am. I claw the slime at the sea bottom but by the time I rise to the surface there is not even silt beneath my fingernails. Ah, but the dive is invigorating! The effort! The work I put in! I will not be defeated *if only I do not quit!* I have re-

turned to the earliest hours of my human existence,
I tell the doctor, when the breast is me and I am the
breast, when all is oneself and oneself is all, when
the concave is the convex and the convex the concave,
my first thousand hours after my aeons of nothing,
the dawn of my life, my Mesopotamia! How I talk!
Anything! Everything! I'll hit upon it yet! I will not
be silent until I am sane! Perhaps it is all a post-analytic
collapse, a year in the making—the most desperate
means I could invent *to cling* to Klinger. "Have you
ever thought, Doctor, what fantasies of dependence
bloom in your childish patients just on the basis of
your name? Have you realized, Doctor, that all our
names begin with K, yours and mine and Kafka's?
And then there is Claire—and Miss Clark!" "The alpha-
bet," he reminds me, a language teacher, "only *has*
twenty-six letters. And there are billions of us in
need of initials for purposes of identification." "But!"
"But what?" "But something! But anything! Please, if
I can't, *you* do it—give me a clue! Give me a lead! I
want to get out of here!"

I try to go over with him the key events of my psychic
life, once again I turn the pages in that anthology of
stories that we two had assembled as a kind of text
for the course we conducted together for five years
in "The History of David Alan Kepesh." But the stories
are of no use, even I have to agree. Too familiar by
now; chewed on once too often already. My life's
drama has all the appeal of some tenth-grade reader

containing Maupassant's "The Necklace" and "The Luck of Roaring Camp." If indeed my own anthology had continued to intrigue me with its density and suggestiveness, I would not have terminated my analysis as I did, but one strong signal, among others, that the project had come to an end was that tales from the life of Kepesh, once as exciting to me as anything in *The Brothers Karamazov*, had been recounted and glossed so many times that finally they were as stale as the favorite literary chestnut of the most retrograde high-school teacher in America. And *that* is a successful analysis.

Ah-hah, thought I. *There's* the trauma that I can't remember: *success itself*. There's what I fled: *my victory*. That's what I couldn't face! "What?" asks Dr. Klinger, "what couldn't you face?" "The rewards! Wholeness! Comfort! A calm and orderly and gratifying life! A life without—" "Wait, wait. Why couldn't you face such things? Those are wonderful things. Come off it, Mr. Kepesh. You could take gratification with the best of them." But I don't listen, since what I hear him saying isn't what he's saying anyway. I talk about what patients talk about, that imaginary friend of the confused, My Guilt. I talk about Helen, my ex-wife, whose life, I understand, is even more horrible now than it was when together we suffered that disaster known as our marriage. For she is married again, to a lush, and from what I hear, has become one herself. I remember how I could not help but gloat several years back when an old friend visiting from San Francisco, where Helen lives once again, told me (and my lovely young mistress, who had cooked our splendid dinner) of Helen's continuing unhappiness, the family slugfests, the twenty-five pounds she's gained, the bags beneath her eyes. Good for the bitch, I thought . . . "And now you think you are punishing yourself with madness for such ordinary, everyday malice? Come off it, Mr. Kepesh." "I'm saying that the prospect of my own happiness was too much for me! That's why the sex began to cool down with Claire, too! So much satisfaction frightened me! Seemed radically unjust! My guilt!" "Oh, come off it, Mr. Kepesh. That is analysis right out of the dime store. Such religiosity. Such self-congratulation in the guise of objective thinking. From a man of your sophistication, no less." "Then if not that, *what*? *Help me! What did it!*"

"Nothing 'did it.' "

"*Then why am I mad?*"

"But you're not."

The next Sunday, when I again ask my father if I am a mental patient—just to be sure—he answers, "No."

"*But last week you said yes!*"

"I was wrong to say that."

"*But it's the truth!*"

"It's not."

"God, I'm reversing again! I'm reversing!"

"You're not," said Dr. Klinger.

"What are *you* doing here? This is Sunday! My father is here, not you! You're not even here!"

"I'm here, Mr. Kepesh. With your father. Right beside you."

"This is all getting confused! I don't want to be confused! Help me! Do you hear me? Help me! I need your help! I cannot do this alone! Lift me! Lift me! Tell me only the truth! If I am a breast where is my milk! When Claire sucks on me, why don't I give milk! Where's my milk! Tell me that!"

"Oh, Davie." It was my father—his unshaven cheek on my areola! "My son, my sonny."

"Daddy, what's happened? Hold me, Poppy—what's happened? *Why did I go mad?*"

"You didn't, darling," he sobbed, his tears dampening my skin.

"*Then where is my milk! Answer me! If I am a breast I would make milk! Hold milk! Swell with milk! And that is too crazy for anybody to believe! Even me! THAT CANNOT BE!*"

But apparently it can be. Just as they are able to increase the milk yield of cows with injections of the lactogenic agent GH, the growth hormone, so it has been hypothesized that I could very possibly become a milk-producing mammary gland with the appropriate hormonal stimulation. There are times now when I want to say, "Go ahead and try, you lying bastards." I am sure there are those in the scientific

67

community who would jump at the chance. Perhaps when I have had enough of this, I will give it to them. And if I am not killed in the process? If they succeed? Well, then I will know that I am madder than anyone has ever been, or else that I am a wholly authentic breast, and not just an endocrine "case" who still answers to the name David Alan Kepesh.

In the meantime, fifteen months have passed—I
accept their figure, why not?—and presently I live
in a state of relative calm. Half of each hour that
Claire spends with me is given over to sensual pleasure,
the rest of the time we talk. She assists me with my
Shakespeare. Yes, of late I have been listening to
recordings of dramatic presentations of the great
tragedies. I began with the Schonbrunns' gift, Olivier
in *Hamlet*. It was here in the room for months before
I asked Mr. Brooks one morning (who turns out to be
a Negro, by the way, so that I see him in my mind's
eye looking like the Senator from Massachusetts),
before I asked Mr. Brooks if he would be so kind as
to put it on the phonograph for me. The fact of the
matter is that ever since college I have been meaning
to reread Shakespeare, but with so much else around
that I hadn't read even once, I had never gotten to it;
it was one of those thousand cultural endeavors that

F

I thought would be "good" for me to undertake "some day." For all I know I may once have said as much to Debbie Schonbrunn, back in our Palo Alto days. And she remembered. If so, it was really as sweetly thoughtful a gift as any she could have chosen. Yet, you will recall, I was so furious with her; well, that just shows, doesn't it, that people are oftentimes made of finer clay than we are willing to grant. On the other hand, there is her husband—enough, enough, he-couldn't-help-it, as the saying goes . . . I spend several hours every morning listening to the records of Laurence Olivier playing Hamlet and Othello, Paul Scofield as Lear, the Old Vic company doing *Macbeth*. Unable to follow along with a text while the play is being spoken, I miss the meaning of an unfamiliar word, or my mind will wander, and when I return I find that for lines on end I am at sea in the syntax and the sense. I make every effort *not* to lose my place, as it were, but despite that effort—that effort! always that effort!—to keep myself firmly fixed on the plight of Shakespeare's heroes, I do continue to consider my own more than I should like to.

The Shakespeare text that I used in college— Neilson and Hill, *The Complete Plays and Poems of William Shakespeare,* bound in blue linen worn thin in places by my earnest undergraduate grip, and heavily underlined by me then for wisdom—is here on the table beside the hammock. It is one of the several books I have asked Claire to bring me from my apartment. I remember so well what it looks like, which in part is why I wanted it here. Claire looks up words in the footnotes and reads to me Elizabethan meanings that I long ago forgot; or she slowly reads aloud some passage that I missed that morning when my mind departed Elsinore Castle for Lenox Hill Hospital. I feel it is important to go over those passages, to "get" them before I go off to sleep. Otherwise it might begin to seem that I listen to *Hamlet* for the same reason that my father answers the phone at my Uncle Larry's catering establishment, to kill the time. In fact I am being as serious about myself as I can.

Olivier is a great man, you know. I have fallen somewhat in love with him, in the manner of a schoolgirl with a movie star. I have never really given my attention over so completely to a genius before, not even in reading. As a student, then a professor, my experience of literature was necessarily contaminated by self-consciousness and the burden of verbalization; either I was learning or I was teaching. But that is behind me, like much else; now I am just listening.

In the beginning I would try to imitate Olivier's manner, and, with all the time I have, managed to memorize whole speeches that I could deliver with his intonation, rhythm, and interpretation. I would recite these speeches for my amusement when I was alone

71

in the evenings. In college I was an actor in plays staged by the dramatic society, and I have always had a talent for mimicry, as well as a small theatrical gift with which, on occasion, I would charm my students. I sounded remarkably like Olivier, I thought, one night when I delivered forth the death scene speech from *Othello*. But then I realized that I was being observed—it was midnight, but nobody has given me a good reason yet why the TV camera should shut down at any hour of the day or night—and so I left off with my imitation. Why should I want to appear any more foolish, or any more pathetic than I already do? I said to myself, "Come now, David, it is all too poignant and heartbreaking, a breast reciting 'And say besides, that in Aleppo once . . .' You will send the scientists home in tears." Bitterness, reader, a shallow sort of bitterness at that, but then permit my dignity a rest, won't you? This is not tragedy any more than it is farce. It is only life, and, like it or not, I am only human.

Did fiction do this to me? "How could it, Mr. Kepesh?" Dr. Klinger asks. No, hormones are hormones and art is art. I did not get this way from falling too strongly under the influence of the great imaginations. "But," I say, "it might be my way of *being* a Kafka, being a Gogol, being a Swift. They could *envision* those marvelous transformations—they were artists. They had the language and those obsessive fictional brains. I didn't. So I had to live the thing."

72

"Had to?" "To achieve *my* art. I had the artistic longing without the necessary detachment. I loved the extreme in literature, idolized those who made it, was fascinated by its imagery and power and suggestiveness—" "And? Yes? The world is full of art lovers—so?" "So I took the leap. Beyond sublimation. I made the word flesh. I have out-Kafkaed Kafka. He could only *imagine* a man turning into a cockroach. But look what I have done." Even I laughed. For where, if I may ask, are the sources of my art? Why Professor David Alan Kepesh of the Department of Comparative Literature of the State University of New York at Stony Brook of all people? But then why Kafka? Why Gogol? Why Swift? They may even have asked themselves that. Why anyone? Great art happens to people like anything else . . . Ah, but I must maintain my perspective. No delusions; certainly no delusions of grandeur.

But if not grandeur, what about frivolity? What about depravity? I could be rich, you know, I could be rich, notorious, and delirious with pleasure for every waking hour of the day. I could call my friend to visit me, the adventurous younger colleague I spoke of earlier. As yet I still have not allowed him here, and not because I fear a repetition of my experience with Arthur Schonbrunn; it isn't irrepressible laughter I'm afraid of now, it's *serious advice*, it's somebody with a new idea of how I should go about living this life. What I am afraid of now is that a visitor will arrive who will tell me that I am out of my mind to lie here in a hammock in this state, being a good brave fellow about it all, listening to records, talking to my analyst, and having thirty minutes per day of some well-bred, well-behaved schoolteacher's idea of hot sex . . . I could call my friend to me then and I could say, "I want to get out of here. We can carry with me whatever pumps and pipes are necessary to sustain me. We can hire as many doctors and nurses as it takes to look after me. I am sick of worrying about losing Claire. Let her go and get a new lover whose sperm she will not drink and lead with him a normal life. I am tired of guarding against the loss of her goodness. And I am tired of my father's maundering too; he bores me. And how much more Shakespeare can I listen to in one life? I realize that all the great plays of Western literature are now available on LPs; I know I could go on to Sophocles, Sheridan, Aristophanes, Shaw, Synge, Racine, et cetera—but to what end? That *is* killing time. For a breast it is the bloody *murder* of time. Pal, I am going to make a great deal of money. I don't think that will be too difficult. If the Beatles can fill Shea Stadium, so can I. We will have to think this through, you and I, but what is all that intelligence of ours for, if not to think such things through? To read more books? I will make hundreds of thousands of dollars. And then I will have girls. I want twelve- and thirteen-year-old girls. I want them three, four, five, and six at a time. I want them licking at my nipple all at once. I want them naked and giggling, stroking and sucking me for days on end. And we can find them, pal, you know that. If the Rolling Stones can find them, if Charles Manson can find them, we can find them too. There will also be women who will want to open their thighs to something as new and thrilling as my nipple. We will be surprised by the number of women, married mothers among them, who will come knocking at the dressing-room door in their chinchillas. Well, we will just have to pick and choose, won't we, select according to beauty, good breeding, and lasciviousness. And I will be deliriously happy. *And I will be deliriously happy.* Remember Gulliver among the Brobdingnags? How the king's maidservants had him walk out on their nipples for the fun of it? *He* didn't think it was fun, poor little fellow. But then he was a humane English physician, a child of the Age of Reason, living quite precariously in an outlandish land of giants; but this, my friend, is the Land of Opportunity in the Age of Self-Fulfillment, and I am David Alan Kepesh, the Breast, and I will live by my own lights!"

"Live by them or die by them?"

"It remains to be seen, Doctor."

Let me conclude the lecture by quoting the esteemed German poet Rainer Maria Rilke. You all know how fond we impassioned and well-meaning literature professors are of ending the hour with something *moving* for the students to carry from the pure-hearted classroom out into the fallen world of dormitories and dope. How could this defrocked teacher resist then, when it may well be that on the basis of his newly begotten fame he has the attention of enormous flocks of sheep as innocent of great poetry as of great catastrophe.

("Fame?" says Dr. Klinger. "Surely the whole world knows by now," I say, "excepting perhaps the Russians and Chinese." "According to your wishes, your case has been handled with ˙all possible secrecy." "But my friends know. The staff here knows—some of them at least. It doesn't take much more than that for a nice grotesque tidbit to spread." "True. But by and large I think that by the time it filters out beyond those close to you, by the time it reaches the man in the street, he tends not to believe it." "He thinks it's a joke." "He thinks it's a story, yes, if, that is, he can take his mind off his own troubles long enough even to listen." "And the media?" "Nothing there, nothing at all." "Now I don't buy that, Dr. Klinger." "Don't. I'm not going to argue. I told you so, long ago, and that should be enough. In the beginning there were inquiries, of course. But they were handled with strict regard for your legally guaranteed right to privacy. Some persisted, but in the end those people have a living to make like everybody else, and they move right along to the next calamity." "Then no one knows all that's happened." "All? No one but you, Mr. Kepesh." "Well, maybe I should be the one to tell them then." "Then you *will* be famous, won't you?" "Better famous by way of the truth than by way of sadistic gossip and crazy tabloid fantasy. Better from me, surely, than from the madmen and the morons out there." "Of course the madmen and the morons out there will get it wrong anyway, you know, regardless of how precise and scrupulous you try to make your report. So you will not be taken on your own terms, ever, you know —this you must realize beforehand." "You mean, I'll always be a joke." "To many, yes. A joke. A grotesque. A charlatan. Of course." "You're advising me, then, to leave well enough alone." "I'm advising you nothing," said Dr. Klinger, "only reminding you of the omnipresence and omnipotence of our old friend with the white beard who sits on the golden throne." "Mr. Reality." "Precisely.")

So then, let me conclude, morons and madmen, tough guys and skeptics, friends, students, relatives, colleagues, and all you strangers, distracted and unblessed, with your billion different fingerprints and faces, let me conclude, my fellow mammalians, with a poem of Rilke's entitled "Archaic Torso of Apollo." Perhaps my story, told here in its entirety for the first time, and with all the truthfulness that is in me, will at the very least illuminate Rilke's great lines for you in a fresh way, particularly his concluding admonition, which is not necessarily as elevated a sentiment as we all might once have liked to believe. Yes, let us proceed with our education, one and all.

We did not know his legendary head,
in which the eyeballs ripened. But
his torso still glows like a candelabrum
in which his gaze, only turned low,

holds and gleams. Else could not the curve
of the breast blind you, nor in the slight turn
of the loins could a smile be running
to that middle, which carried procreation.

Else would this stone be standing maimed and short
under the shoulders' translucent plunge
nor flimmering like the fell of beasts of prey

nor breaking out of all its contours
like a star: for there is no place
that does not see you. You must change your life.

170773WRL